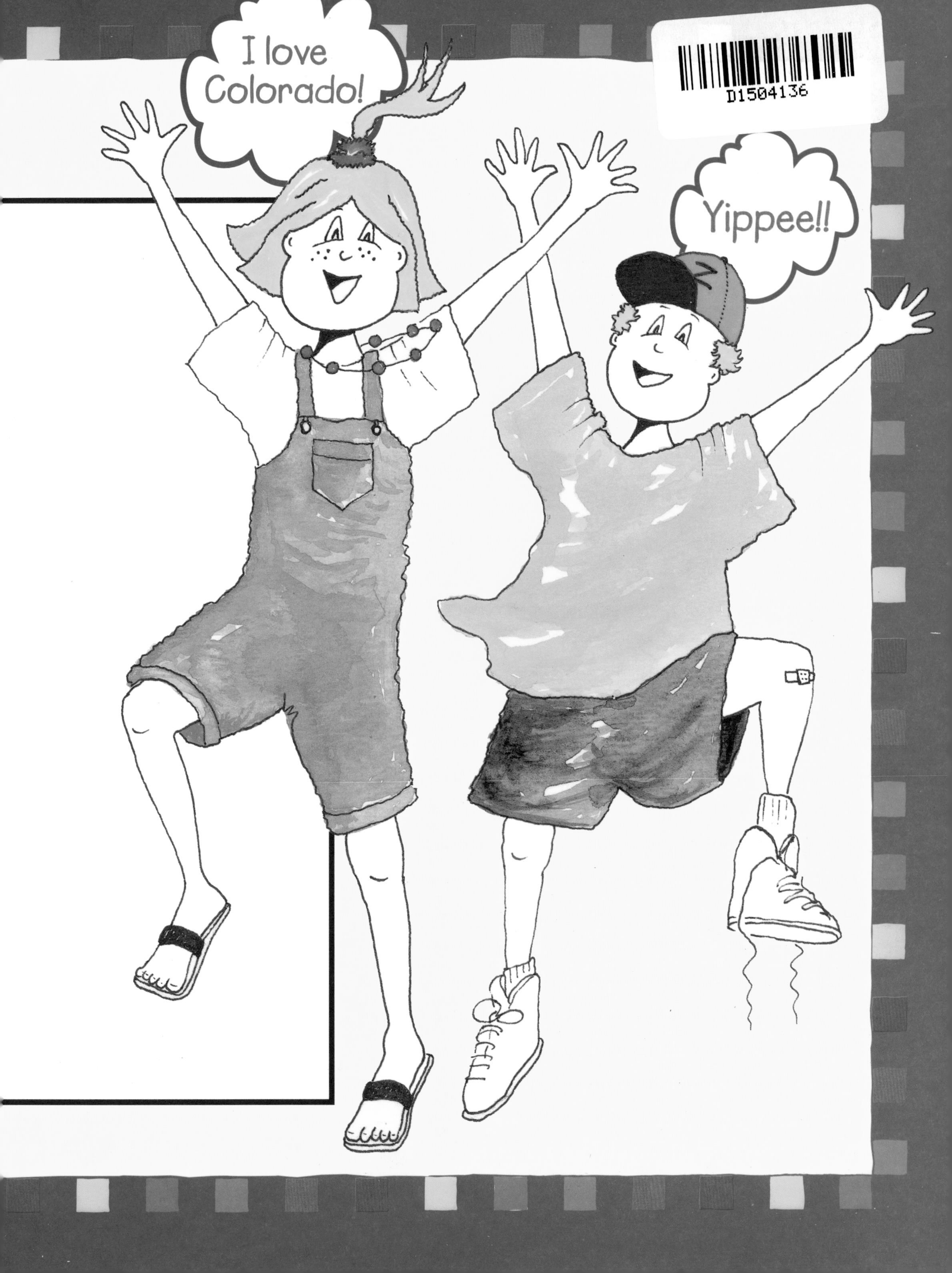
I love Colorado!
Yippee!!

To Kinsey,
I hope you have
lots of cool Colorado
adventures of your own!

Julie Danneberg

Margaret's Magnificent Colorado Adventure

Written by Julie Danneberg

Illustrated by Ian Paton

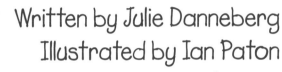

kids
WESTCLIFFE PUBLISHERS

Dear Margaret,

I hope you have a wonderful time on your trip to Colorado. If you write in this journal and share with us everything that you do, see, and learn, you won't have to do any make-up work when you get back to school.

Ms. McGuire

Dedication:
To Alex, Jack, and Walker, my favorite traveling companions. — JD

For Amy, Emily, Will, and Astro (our dog, who also likes road trips). — IP

COLORADO

Denver

DAY 1
DENVER

Dear Ms. McGuire,

Thank you for this journal. I'm **excited** to start writing about my trip. At first I felt a little strange about writing something the whole class was going to read, but then my mom said to pretend that I'm writing to a friend. So that is what I'm going to do!

Right now we are jetting our way to Colorado. When we get there, Dad says we are going to take our time and see the state. I hope we get to Denver **soon.** When I look out the window all I see are clouds, clouds, and more clouds.

boring!!

I'M GOING NUTS!

Hey, do you guys want to meet my family?

This is my dad: He's kind of funny—but he loves to embarrass me in front of my friends. Usually he does it on purpose, but sometimes he does it without even trying.

My mom is pretty cool, too. She loves going to new places and learning new things. However, her idea of a great time is going to the library.

You already know me, Margaret. Practically **perfect.**

Zack, my younger brother, is practically **imperfect** in every way: loud, obnoxious, and very immature.

Well, now you know all about us. And just in time, too. The pilot said we are about ready to land. Denver, Colorado, **here we come!!!**

Dear Grandma,
We made it safe and sound. Denver International Airport is totally cool, especially from the air. It looks like a village of white teepees. Zack already spent the money you gave him—on a **rock!**

Love from your favorite grandchild,
Margaret

Grandma
1010 John's Field
Cookieland, GA 11090

Hey! Who turned out the lights?

om and Dad rented a van. They said we needed more room to spread out. (The truth is that they think Zack and I will fight.)

It's a gorgeous, sunny day. Good thing I brought my sunglasses and sunscreen. Zack forgot his, but I've thought of the perfect solution—a paper bag!

Who says recycling isn't fun?

We had the whole afternoon to explore, so we started at the Colorado History Museum. We learned that in the summer of 1858, a prospector panning close to the confluence of the South Platte River and Cherry Creek found a few flakes of gold that had washed down from the mountains. **You know what?** That tiny bit of gold **started** the Colorado gold rush. Miners, on the way to the mountains, stopped in Denver for equipment, supplies, and whiskey. Prospectors stopped back in Denver to spend their hard-earned gold on dancing, gambling, and more whiskey.

On our way out we stopped at the museum store. We didn't find whiskey, but Mom bought a book and Zack bought... a **rock.**

Cool!

Another rock?!

Amethyst

What next?

After a lot of discussion and a little bit of arguing, we decided on the United States Mint. That's where the United States government makes money. Did you know that there are only **four** mints in the whole United States?

When it opened in 1863, the Mint melted gold dust and gold nuggets into heavy gold bars. Now, the Mint can make 35 to 40 million coins in a day. Every coin made here gets a D stamped on the front. Look at your coins. **Are any of them made in Denver?** Maybe they were minted on the day my family visited.

I'm rich!

FUN FACT:
The U.S. Mint in Denver can produce up to 10 billion coins a year.

Sightseeing is hard work.

ZZZ

DAY 2
COLORADO SPRINGS

On the way to Colorado Springs, I saw Pike's Peak, one of Colorado's most famous fourteeners. Actually, at a height of 14,110 feet, Pike's Peak is hard to miss. Zebulon Pike, one of the first white men to explore this region, thought it impossible to climb. Wrong! Now tourists can drive, hike, or take a train to the top.

We took the cog train. At the summit I said to Zack, **"Aren't these spacious skies beautiful?"** and **"Check out the purple mountain's majesty."**

"Margaret, you're weird," he answered.

Maybe so, but at least I recognize the words from the song, **"America the Beautiful."** Katherine Lee Bates wrote those words after she visited Pike's Peak in 1893.

Before we left we visited the gift shop. Zack bought— what else?— a **rock.**

Another rock? The kid is definitely **not** my brother.

Rocks are awesome!

Cog Train

Jasper

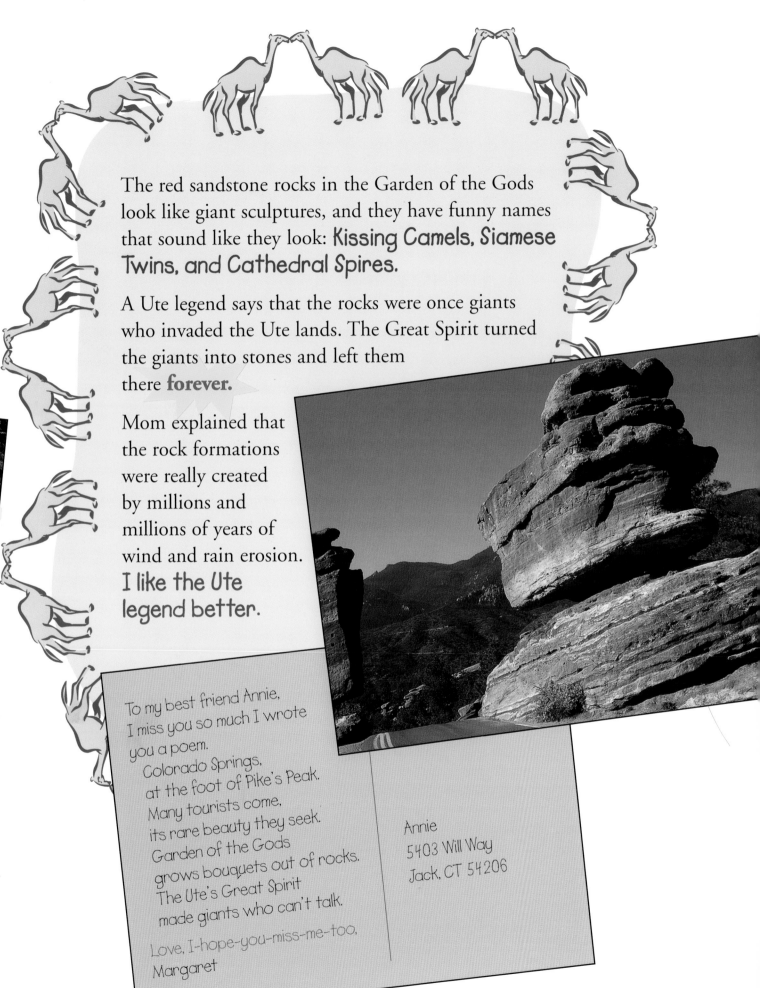

The red sandstone rocks in the Garden of the Gods look like giant sculptures, and they have funny names that sound like they look: **Kissing Camels, Siamese Twins, and Cathedral Spires.**

A Ute legend says that the rocks were once giants who invaded the Ute lands. The Great Spirit turned the giants into stones and left them there **forever.**

Mom explained that the rock formations were really created by millions and millions of years of wind and rain erosion. **I like the Ute legend better.**

To my best friend Annie,
I miss you so much I wrote you a poem.
   Colorado Springs,
     at the foot of Pike's Peak.
   Many tourists come,
     its rare beauty they seek.
   Garden of the Gods
     grows bouquets out of rocks.
   The Ute's Great Spirit
     made giants who can't talk.

Love, I-hope-you-miss-me-too,
Margaret

Annie
5403 Will Way
Jack, CT 54206

We walked around on nature trails, kicking up red dust and sending grasshoppers flying. The sun beamed down so hot that Mom made me wear her hat. **YUK!**

I was glad to get to our campground. Mom and Dad set up our tent. It took them forever. **Are tents supposed to sag in the middle?**

The tent is really small. It didn't look big enough to hold all of us. I told Zack he'd have to sleep outside. He threw my sleeping bag out of the tent. What a brat!

And stay out!

MARGARET'S TRAVEL TIP:

When chocolate lovers carry the chocolate for the s'mores, you will probably end up with **s'minuses.**

We cooked hotdogs and for dessert we had s'mores— my favorite! The only problem? Dad had already eaten most of the chocolate. Now I know why he let us go ahead of him on our hike.

Right now, it's dark and I'm writing by the light of the campfire. It snaps, crackles, and pops. I do have one worry, though. What if I have to go to the bathroom in the middle of the night?!

DAY 3
ROYAL GORGE TO GUNNISON

This morning, we hadn't been driving for more than five minutes before Zack got out all of his toys and car snacks. I can't believe how much **junk** he hauls around in his backpack. The car stunk when he took off his shoes. Phew! Mom needs to make that kid take a **bath!**

WHAT IN THE WORLD IS IN ZACK'S BACKPACK?

Zack says:

Margaret says:

Zack says:		Margaret says:
Gold coins		Bottle caps
Rattlesnake		Piece of rope
Sword		Stick
Treasures		Rocks

The Royal Gorge is pretty **gorge-ous.** (Get it?) You should see how deep this canyon is. A suspension bridge crosses over the top, with the Arkansas River far below. Instead of being built up from the ground like most bridges, it hangs **suspended** from two 300-ton cables.

Looking out over the edge of the canyon, Zack wanted to throw a rock, but Mom and Dad said no. While they weren't looking, he spit a big, white, sloppy spitball instead. We watched it disappear into the canyon.

(I'm glad there wasn't anyone below!)

FUN FACT:
The *Royal Gorge Bridge* is the world's highest suspension bridge. San Francisco's Golden Gate Bridge is also a suspension bridge.

Driving over Monarch Pass after lunch, Mom told us we had just crossed the Continental Divide, a chain of high mountains stretching from Canada to Mexico that cuts the continent in half. On the west side of the mountain, water from rain or melting snow runs toward the Pacific Ocean.

On the east, water runs to the Gulf of Mexico. Just think, two raindrops falling close to each other on the top of this mountain could end up on different sides of the United States!

We drove to Gunnison, on the other side of Monarch Pass. It's a great place to fish and hunt. As we unpacked at our hotel, Dad reached behind the luggage and pulled out a fishing pole and a jar of bait. "Anyone want to catch a fish?" he asked.

He didn't have to ask twice. We took turns fishing next to a wide, slow-moving stretch of the Gunnison River. We tried our best, but believe me — fishing is harder than it looks!

Finally, Zack caught a rainbow trout. Dad wanted to cook it. Zack wanted to keep it, and I wanted to throw it back. "We don't have a pan or a bucket, so back it goes," Mom said, flipping the trout into the river. (I love it when I'm right!)

Dear Uncle Walker,
Guess what we did today? Caught a great big **rainbow trout**. It was huge, almost as big as me! We let it go after Mom took pictures. I'm glad. It smelled!

Say hi to all my cousins,
Margaret

Uncle Walker
1515 Alex Road
Fish, IL 66391

DAY 4
BLACK CANYON

We left Gunnison early this morning and drove to the Black Canyon of the Gunnison National Monument. Although the Black Canyon is 53 miles long, the 13 miles that make up the monument are especially **dark and deep.** For two million years, bit by tiny bit, the Gunnison River cut deeper and deeper through the rocks.

Tourists can visit the north rim or the south rim. We stopped at an overlook on the north rim: a deck with thick log railings and nothing but sheer cliff below. When I looked down, my stomach did **flips, rolypolys, and somersaults** all at once. We were up so high we saw birds flying below us!

In some places the Black Canyon walls are 2,425 feet deep. That is equal to almost eight Statues of Liberty stacked end to end.

Nice hair, Margaret!

Later we hiked down to the bottom of the canyon. Mom called it a **backwards hike** because we did the easy part first. Yellow, red, and purple wildflowers looked bright next to the black canyon walls towering above us.

The trail followed a little creek that turned into a waterfall as it cascaded downhill to join the Gunnison River.

At the bottom we picnicked beside the river. Zack and I threw rocks into the water, sailed log boats through the rapids, and jumped from rock to rock. **"Be careful,"** Dad warned. **Too late.** My foot slipped off the rock and I stood ankle deep in **icy cold river water.** For the rest of the hike I squished when I walked. **Zack called me the Creature from the Black Canyon.** Not funny!

At the visitor center, Zack bought— you guessed it— another rock!

Sulphur

17

It was late afternoon before we started out for Ouray. Nicknamed the **Switzerland of America,** Ouray is completely surrounded by towering grey mountains. It's a small town, started in **1876** after a gold strike. **I don't think much has changed since then.** The stores on the main street have false wooden fronts, and the Victorian houses look like something out of a fairy tale.

At the bookstore, Mom bought a book on the town's history and I bought a postcard. There weren't any rocks so **Zack pouted** and Dad bought him a postcard of the Rocky Mountains.

Hey, no fair!

Ouray

No rocks. No fun!!

Mom told me about the Ute Indian Chief, **Ouray.** The Utes lived and hunted in this part of Colorado for hundreds of years. That is, until gold was found. After that, the white settlers wanted this land for themselves.

Chief Ouray tried to protect the Ute land while still keeping peace. Eventually, though, all the Utes were pushed off their land and sent to reservations.

Hey, that's really no fair! **What a sad story.**

Chief Ouray and his wife, Chipeta, traveled to Washington, D.C. in 1874 to meet with President Grant about protecting the Ute land.

Stacy,
Tonight we walked around the town of Ouray. The cold air smelled good — like cozy fires and winter. A million stars sparkled in the night sky. They seem closer in the mountains. I wanted to reach up and take one to send home to you.

Missing you,
Margaret

Stacy
1010 Emily Place
Sean, KY 00473

DAY 5
OURAY

This morning, Zack woke up real early again. Boy, that boy bugs me!

As we walked to the Box Canyon Falls, **I heard a loud, rumbling noise.** When we got there, a wooden sidewalk, built into the rock walls of the canyon, led us right up next to the waterfall. The water shot through a hole in the rock, and then fell 285 feet to the river below. A misty spray of water **drenched** me, and I felt the noise of the waterfall down through my feet.

Are you awake?

Underground Mine

Ventilation Shaft

Shaft

Ore Body

CHILD TICKET

BACHELOR-SYRACUSE MINE TOUR

Ouray, Colorado

Tour Admission $4.95

After lunch, we took a tour of the Bachelor-Syracuse Mine, **a real gold and silver mine.** We wore hard hats and yellow rain slickers and rode a tiny train called a trammer 3,350 feet, over half a mile, into the mine.

The guide showed us a miner's hat.
He said that miners are used to the dark.
Then he shut off all the lights. The mine
was **pitch black and very scary!**
I didn't like it one bit.

Annie,
We went in an old mine. Water
dripped from the ceiling and walls
into muddy puddles on the ground.
The cool air smelled musty. A few
lightbulbs let off a spooky glow.
I couldn't help but think of the
tall mountain towering above me.
I felt very small.

From, Never-could-be-a-miner,
Margaret

Annie
5403 Will Way
Jack, CT 54206

DAY 6

DURANGO

Our drive over Red Mountain Pass **almost gave me a heart attack** — too curvy, windy, and high up for me! We got to the old mining town of Silverton just in time to watch the Durango and Silverton Narrow Gauge Railroad chug into town. The train, with its bright orange passenger cars, starts in Durango and turns around in Silverton. The cars and engine are just like they used to be years and years ago. Mom said that looking at the train was like looking at a piece of living history. **What can I say?** She gets all excited about things like that.

I can't look down. Ohhhhh!

Durango and Silverton Narrow Gauge Railroad

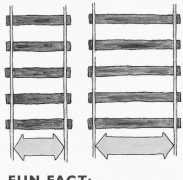

FUN FACT:
Narrow gauge railroad tracks are 3 feet apart. Regular railroad tracks are about 4 feet 8 inches apart.

Durango, our last stop of the day, is definitely **a real western town.** I expected to see a gunslinger ride in on his way to the saloon, or a prospector trudging by with his donkey. Driving into town, I did see license plates from Maine, Utah, California, and Tennessee. I heard people talking French, Spanish, German, and Swedish.

FUN FACT:
A lot of Hollywood westerns were filmed in this area. "Butch Cassidy and the Sundance Kid," "True Grit," and "City Slickers" were filmed nearby.

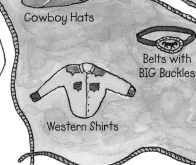

(SOME OF) THE THINGS THEY SELL IN DURANGO

Cowboy Hats

Belts with BIG Buckles

Western Shirts

Pink Tutus (huh?)

Cowboy Boots

25

I also heard a little-known language called **Zackanese.** That is the special language spoken by an obnoxious younger brother trying to get his parents to buy him more rocks.

Right now, the only language I understand is "Good-night." **It's been a long day and I'm pooped!**

Stacy,
Tonight we went to a melodrama. This is my kind of play — the audience is supposed to make noise! While we booed and hissed, clapped and cheered, the good guy saved the lady-in-distress from the bad guy. Zack even blew her a kiss.

From,
I-want-to-be-an-actress,
Margaret

Stacy
1010 Emily Plac
Sean, KY 0047

When does the fun start?

When it's over!

DAY 7
RAFTING

One reason people come to Durango, besides the scenery, is to have **fun.** We decided to take a raft trip along the Animas River. My favorite part? The rapids, of course! The rubber boat flew up and tipped one way and then another. The water spilled over, getting us sopping wet. Zack and I screamed our heads off! Mom got a picture of Zack dressed in his river gear. He thought he was cool, calling himself **AquaDude** all day. Aqua Dud is more like it!

MARGARET'S TRAVEL TIP: Don't go on a river raft trip if you want to maintain your image.

Ahhh!

Weee!

Ohhh!

Omph. Maybe I'll just stay down here.

Another early morning. We wanted to have plenty of time to spend at Mesa Verde National Park. Mom told us all about the history of the Ancient Puebloans who once lived here. When they first came about 1,400 years ago, they hunted wild animals and gathered plants, nuts, and berries.

After awhile they became farmers, growing their own food on the mesa tops. Since they didn't have to move around as much, they built bigger, better, more permanent houses — the cliff dwellings.

Then, something strange happened. All at once they disappeared. No one knows for sure where they went or why. (Sometimes I wish Zack would make like an "ancient one" and disappear himself!)

FUN FACT:
Archaeologists believe that the Pueblo Indians, like the Hopi in Arizona, are descendants of the ancient cliffdwellers. Therefore, Ancient Puebloans is a more correct name than Anasazi, which is a Navajo word.

Awesome!

Spruce Tree House is another cliff dwelling. As I explored, I pictured the Ancient Puebloans' life. Women grinding corn. Men sitting on balconies. Children, dogs, and turkeys running around making noises and getting in everyone's way. For a minute, I forgot all the tourists.

Then Zack called, "Come on, Margaret!" I followed him as he scrambled down a ladder into a kiva, the place where religious ceremonies were held. Inside, I found a circular room, dark except for the square of light filtering in from the roof-hole.

Is dinner ready?

From Spruce Tree House, we followed a trail into the canyon. The rocky path wound around the base of the sandstone cliffs, and it was very quiet except for the buzz of insects. Above us, four black ravens dipped and swooped, calling to each other. Mom pointed out a **tiny lizard sunning on a rock.**

Finally we came to petroglyphs carved on a rock wall. Archaeologists don't know what the geometric signs and figures say, but that doesn't matter to me. All I know is that hundreds of years ago someone stood in this very spot and **"spoke."** Now, I am here to "listen."

I didn't want to leave Mesa Verde. "I'll be back," I whispered to myself as we drove out of the park.

ZZZZZ

Oh no! My hair! My beautiful hair!

OOPS!!

MARGARET'S TRAVEL TIP: Don't sit in front of someone blowing bubbles!

There is a saying in Colorado: If you don't like the weather, **wait a minute.** I thought up my own saying: If you don't like the scenery, **drive a mile.** I'm not kidding! On the drive from Mesa Verde to Grand Junction, we passed mesas, mountains, tall cliffs, and farmland. Just when I got bored looking at one kind of landscape, it changed.

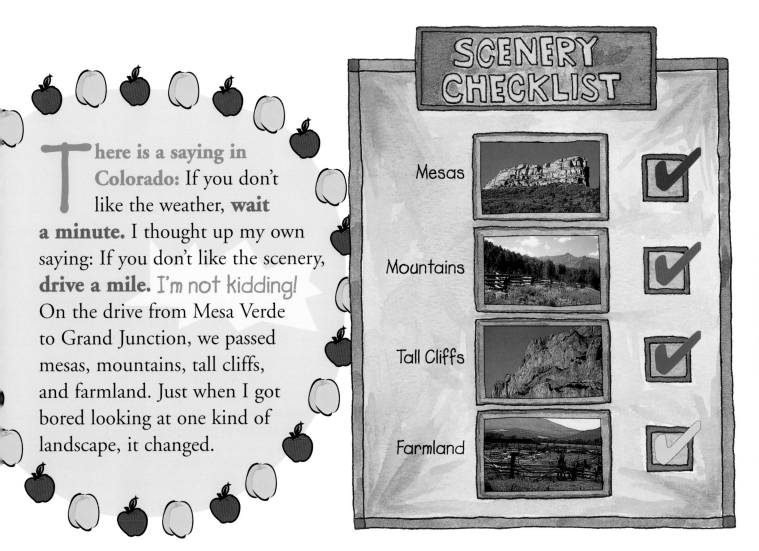

SCENERY CHECKLIST

Mesas ✔

Mountains ✔

Tall Cliffs ✔

Farmland ✔

Grand Junction is famous for its peaches, apples, and pears. We saw fruit and vegetable stands everywhere. Finally Dad said, **"I can't stand it any longer,"** and he stopped to buy a bushel basket of peaches. They were the best. We ate most of them right then and there, and didn't even care that we had peach juice dripping off our chins, down our arms, and between our fingers. Zack said it was like eating a peach pie without the crust.

FRESH FRUIT

PEACHES

PEARS

APPLES

PEACHES

PEARS

31

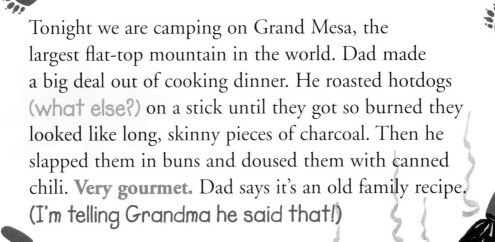

Tonight we are camping on Grand Mesa, the largest flat-top mountain in the world. Dad made a big deal out of cooking dinner. He roasted hotdogs (what else?) on a stick until they got so burned they looked like long, skinny pieces of charcoal. Then he slapped them in buns and doused them with canned chili. **Very gourmet.** Dad says it's an old family recipe. (I'm telling Grandma he said that!)

Dear Grandma,
Dad burned the hotdogs again! We need to teach this guy how to cook!

From, I-never-eat-burned-food, Margaret

Grandma
555 Nathan Ridge
Hotdog, WI 03529

DAY 9

GLENWOOD SPRINGS

Before we hit the road this afternoon, we stopped for a snack. Dad calls it **road food,** Mom calls it **junk food,** Zack and I just call it good eatin'. Zack got a candy bar, I got cookies, and Dad got a bag of licorice. We washed it down with a big pop. Mom said we were eating too much sugar.

Dad laughed. **"How can you have too much sugar?"** he asked.

I agree!

DAD'S 4 BASIC FOOD GROUPS

Potato Chips

Licorice

Candy Bars

Pop

WELCOME TO GLENWOOD SPRINGS

It took us about an hour to drive to Glenwood Springs, a town famous for its hot springs. Mom explained that hot springs have **boiling hot water** that bubbles right up from inside the earth. The Ute Indians believed that this water had **special healing powers** and that bathing in it helped them become better hunters and warriors.

Glenwood Hot Springs Pool

Zack and I had **fun** swimming at the Glenwood Hot Springs Pool. There are two pools filled with real hot spring water. One is medium-sized and very, very **hot.** The other is humongous and **warm.** First, we cooked ourselves in the hot pool and then we cooled ourselves off in the other pool. **Back and forth, back and forth we ran.** That is, until we noticed the "bubble chairs" in the hot pool. They looked like underwater lounge chairs. **We begged to try one.** Finally, Dad said **okay.** Zack and I squeezed into a chair. **We jiggled and jounced until it got dark outside.** Then we played hide-and-seek in the steam until our fingers and toes looked like **shrivelled-up raisins!**

MARGARET'S TRAVEL TIP:
Be nice to little brothers who use cameras. Especially if the bathroom in your hotel room doesn't have a lock.

Close the door!

Hee, hee, hee!

Who decided we weren't going to sleep late on this vacation? And is it a vacation if you never get to sleep in? I asked Dad these questions when the alarm went off before dawn this morning, but he just told me to **stop grumbling** and get in the car.

We started out, in the dim morning light, for Breckenridge. Most people come here to ski, hike, and enjoy the mountains. **Not us.** We rented prospectors' gold pans and panned for gold in the Blue River.

Actually, it's not as easy as it looks. The water and sand are supposed to slosh out of the pan, leaving the heavier gold behind. My water sloshed out all right. **All over me!** Pretty soon, Zack's water sloshed over me, too. So of course, I swished some his way. We were on the way to a major waterfight when Zack jumped up and down yelling, "**I'm rich! I'm rich!**" He found a gold nugget in the bottom of his pan. I saw one in my pan, too. Mom winked at me so I knew they weren't real, but for a few seconds **I felt myself coming down with a bad case of gold fever!**

Zack put his gold nugget in with his other rocks. **This time I don't blame him.** This is a rock I want to save, too.

FUN FACT:
Thirteen pounds is the size of "Tom's Baby," Colorado's largest gold nugget found near Breckenridge.

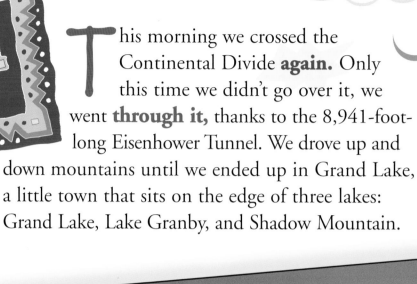

DAY 11
GRAND LAKE

This morning we crossed the Continental Divide **again.** Only this time we didn't go over it, we went **through it,** thanks to the 8,941-foot-long Eisenhower Tunnel. We drove up and down mountains until we ended up in Grand Lake, a little town that sits on the edge of three lakes: Grand Lake, Lake Granby, and Shadow Mountain.

FUN FACT:
Grand Lake is Colorado's largest natural lake.

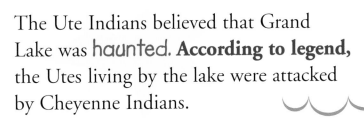

The Ute Indians believed that Grand Lake was haunted. **According to legend,** the Utes living by the lake were attacked by Cheyenne Indians.

To protect the women and children, Ute warriors put them on boats and pushed them out onto the water. A sudden storm came up, the boats tipped, and all the women and children drowned. After that, the Utes named the lake **Spirit Lake** and stayed away from it.

We rented a canoe, but after Zack heard that story, he didn't want to row out onto the lake with me. I guess he wasn't spirited enough. (Spirited, get it? That's a good one, don't you think?)

Grand Lake

Dear Annie,
Tonight I feel like a real pioneer woman. We are staying in a rustic log cabin. From my bed I can look up and see the stars through the cracks in the roof.

From,
I-hope-it-doesn't-rain,
Margaret

Annie
5403 Will Way
Jack, CT 54206

Driving over Trail Ridge Road in Rocky Mountain National Park this morning got my heart pumping. It's fifty miles long and eleven of those miles are above timberline! You know what that means, don't you? For eleven miles we were above 11,000 feet. Aaaggghhh! Even trees don't grow up this high. I should have packed my parachute!

Trail Ridge Road

FUN FACT:
More than 900 different types of wildflowers are found in Rocky Mountain National Park.

Dear Uncle Dan,
Rocky Mountain National Park is incredible! Big, too. It covers 415 square miles. That's one-fourth the size of the state of Rhode Island. It has more than 300 miles of trails. Even Mom and Dad couldn't do that much hiking.
See you soon,
Margaret

Uncle Dan
1515 Ande's Walk
Harlene, IL 66391

Before we went exploring, we drove to the campground and Mom and Dad set up the tent.

From the campground we hiked a trail that took us up to a mountaintop. The park ranger told us that being up on the alpine tundra in Rocky Mountain National Park is like being in the **Arctic regions by the North Pole.** I told Zack that the alpine tundra of Rocky Mountain National Park is **where Santa comes for his summer vacation** (well, it could be true!).

Rocky Mountain National Park

DAY 13

ESTES PARK

Dad said we couldn't finish our trip without seeing a little of Colorado the pioneer way — **by horseback.** So, in Estes Park we did just that. My horse was named Moonlight and Zack's was named Scooter. But we called him Stinker. *Can you guess why?*

We rode way up into the mountains, far away from the crowds. I heard the clip-clop of our horses' hooves and the woosh of the wind through the pines. Above me towered ragged, gray peaks. Now I know what all of Colorado looked like a long time ago.

After our ride, when we got off our horses, my bottom hurt and Zack walked funny.

MARGARET'S TRAVEL TIP:
Don't offer to carry someone's backpack if they collect rocks for a hobby.

Thanks for your help, Margaret.

For the last night of our trip, we stayed in Estes Park in the fancy, old Stanley Hotel (built in 1909). Dad said, "We saved the best for last."

"Personally," I said, "I think our whole trip has been the best!"

FUN FACT:
Freelan Stanley, the man who built the Stanley Hotel, also invented the kerosene-powered Stanley Steamer automobile in 1899.

45

DAY 14

HEADING HOME

This morning we packed for the trip home. I felt sorry for the baggage handlers when they lifted Zack's bag filled with rocks and Mom's bag of books. And poor Dad, he didn't collect anything! But he said he did collect something — **good memories.**

Can't wait to get home!

Where to next?

CHIPS

Pike's Peak

Red Mountain Pass

Box Canyon Falls

Cliff Palace

MARGARET'S TRAVEL TIP: Keep a travel journal. It's a blast!

I agree. We had a **great** time traveling through Colorado. I'm not sure which was my favorite part. I liked the mountains, and I liked hiking, and I really liked Mesa Verde. I even thought it was okay to share a room, or a tent, with Mom, Dad, and Zack — but don't tell them I said that.

I've decided that Colorado is a perfectly magnificent place to go for a vacation... even if you have to bring your brother along!

Dear Margaret,

Your travel journal is fantastic. Thanks for sharing. I felt like I was right there with you on your vacation. Although, I must admit, the raft trip sounded a little too wet and scary for me!

I'm sorry Zack can't share his rock collection with us. Tell him not to give up hope. Maybe the airline will find his luggage after all.

I'm glad to hear that you are already planning your next trip. Arizona sounds like fun. I can't wait to hear all about that trip, too! Who knows, maybe next year Zack will be in my class. (But I'll sure miss you, Margaret.)

Ms. McGuire
P.S. You earned an **A+.**

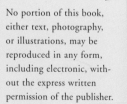

kids WESTCLIFFE PUBLISHERS

For more information about other fine books and calendars from Westcliffe Publishers, please call your local bookstore, contact us at 1-800-523-3692, or write for our free color catalog.

COVER PHOTO:
San Juan Mountains
Courtesy of John Fielder

LIBRARY OF CONGRESS CATALOGING-IN-PUBLICATION DATA:

Danneberg, Julie, 1958–
  Margaret's magnificent Colorado adventure / by Julie Danneberg ; [illustrated by Ian Paton].
    p. cm.
  Summary : Margaret records in her journal the many wondrous sites she and her family visit on their vacation to Colorado, including the Garden of the Gods, the Royal Gorge, the Continental Divide, and the Black Canyon.
  ISBN: 1-56579-329-3
  [1. Colorado—Fiction. 2. Vacations—Fiction. 3. Diaries—Fiction.] I. Paton, Ian, 1959– ill. II. Title.
PZ7.D2327Mar 1999   98-31232
[Fic]—dc21   CIP
                                     AC

ISBN: 1-56579-329-3

TEXT COPYRIGHT:
Julie Danneberg, 1999. All rights reserved.

ILLUSTRATION COPYRIGHT:
Ian Paton, 1999. All rights reserved.

PHOTOGRAPHY COPYRIGHT:
Ian Paton, 1999. All rights reserved.
Bruce Paton, 1999. All rights reserved.

EDITOR: Kristen Iversen

PRODUCTION MANAGER: Craig Keyzer

DESIGN AND PRODUCTION:
Rebecca Finkel, F + P Graphic Design

PUBLISHED BY: Westcliffe Publishers, Inc.
P.O. Box 1261, Englewood, Colorado 80150

PRINTED IN: Hong Kong by H & Y Printing, Ltd.

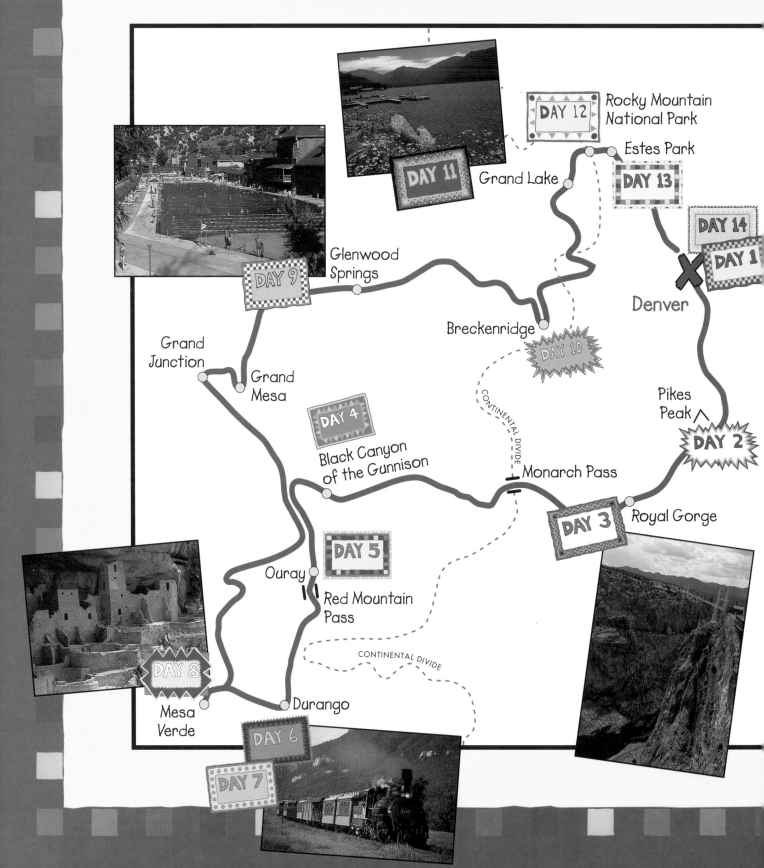

COLORADO

DAY 12 — Rocky Mountain National Park

DAY 11

Grand Lake — Estes Park

DAY 13

DAY 14

DAY 1

Denver

Glenwood Springs

DAY 9

Breckenridge

DAY 10

Grand Junction

Grand Mesa

Pikes Peak

DAY 4

CONTINENTAL DIVIDE

DAY 2

Black Canyon of the Gunnison

Monarch Pass

DAY 3 — Royal Gorge

DAY 5

Ouray

Red Mountain Pass

CONTINENTAL DIVIDE

DAY 8

Mesa Verde

Durango

DAY 6

DAY 7